The Littlest Red Horse

Written by Charles Tazewell • Illustrated by Frank Sofo

Ideals Children's Books • Nashville, Tennessee
an imprint of Hambleton-Hill Publishing

Published by Ideals Children's Books
An imprint of Hambleton-Hill Publishing, Inc.
1501 County Hospital Road
Nashville, Tennessee 37218
800-327-5113

Library of Congress Cataloging-in-Publication Data
Tazewell, Charles.
        The Littlest Red Horse / written by Charles Tazewell ;
illustrated by Frank Sofo. --1st ed.
        p. cm.
        Summary: Having helped a very sick boy have adventures by taking
him to special places all over the world, the merry-go-round horse
called the Littlest Red Horse helps him get into Heaven.
        ISBN 1-57102-157-4 (hardcover)
        [1. Horses—Fiction. 2. Merry-go-round—Fiction. 3. Sick—Fiction.]
I. Sofo, Frank, ill. II. Title.
        PZ7.T219Lk 1999
[E]—dc21   99-37289
                                                                CIP

First Edition
10 9 8 7 6 5 4 3 2 1

To my wife Vincenza for her loving support.
And to my high school buddies, Bob, Alex, and Ray, wherever you are.
—F.S.

Except for his color, there is no discernible difference in appearance between the Littlest Red Horse and his brothers of yellow and pink and green and lavender. His eyes are no brighter; his mane is no more luxuriant. He is but one of the twenty-four fleet, handsome steeds that adorn the merry-go-round of Esteban Gomez.

Still, sooner or later the Littlest Red Horse claims the attention of every visitor to the carnival lot, for he seems to be composed of one quarter magic, one quarter dreams-come-true, one quarter happiness and one quarter mystery. No child astride his back ever fails to catch the lucky brass ring for a free ride.

Any little girl, no matter how plain, who chooses him for her mount, seems to be suddenly and strangely blessed with beauty. Any boy who straddles him seems to change from a freckled, toothless, squirming, noisy rider to a perfect little gentleman, if only for the instant he rides. Cotton floss candy and ice cream cones never melt away at the touch of a tongue of one who sits upon the back of the Littlest Red Horse!

One day, on a blacktop road in the early morning hours, when night was night and morning was morning but neither of them had met, the truck of Esteban Gomez, carrying his dismantled merry-go-round to the next town, slid off the shoulder of the road and skidded dangerously around.

Luckily neither Esteban nor the truck suffered serious damage; he was soon back on the road and on his way. As he drove along, Esteban gave thanks for the protection of his life and property. It was gratifying to know that the angels were not tied down to the forty-hour week. Every minute of the day or night, they were insuring the safety of all travel, whether it be horizontal, vertical or whirling about in a circle on a merry-go-round.

However, when Esteban reassembled his merry-go-round on the carnival lot, he learned to his horror that he had but twenty-three horses when he should have had a galloping two dozen. It was the pink . . . no, no, it was the yellow . . . no, it was the Littlest Red Horse that was missing!

Esteban drove back to the scene of the accident. He searched and searched— but could not find the Littlest Red Horse. He did discover some hoof marks that led to an irrigation ditch; but there they ended, just as though their owner had given a prodigious and final leap and vanished completely.

It was a black moment for Esteban. He had suffered a grievous loss. The  Littlest Red Horse was his favorite, though he would never in a trillion years admit it; and so Esteban, driving carefully because the steering wheel was slick with his tears, drove off, believing in his heart that the Littlest Red Horse had dissolved into thin air.

At that exact moment, the Littlest Red Horse was fast asleep under a bed in a hospital. Earlier, when he became conscious and saw Esteban drive away, he was happy his master was not hurt. However, he felt he might need medical attention. Although he seemed to be whole in every respect, he thought something internal might be wrong.

So after he had chased coyotes, raced a speeding train and beat it, kicked and entered a harness shop and tried on all the silver-mounted saddles, buffed and waxed himself at a car wash, and discussed merry-go-rounds with an over-worked hobby horse, he entered the hospital and rolled under the nearest bed, soon falling fast asleep.

A while later, he was half-awakened by two modulated voices that threw such words as tonsillectomy, appendectomy, and acetaminophen back and forth to each other as though they had no more weight than ping-pong balls. The Littlest Red Horse lifted his head when he thought the heaviest voice said, "Devon," because he remembered Esteban saying what a lovely place that was. When he learned that the place they were talking about was "Heaven" and that they were sending all their prayers there, he promptly lost interest. They made it sound like such a sad place. He never intended to go to any place sad because a merry-go-round just didn't go to such places.

The Littlest Red Horse came wide awake when the lighter voice mentioned the name "Edward." He had known many Edwards and had found them to be very nice people. So, he resolved, when the hospital quieted down for the night, he would seek out this Edward, find out if he knew him, and perhaps have a nice chat about old times.

He slept away the rest of the day and evening; then when it was late and the hospital was still, the Littlest Red Horse made a tour of the wards. He found several Sams, lots of Bills, plenty of Joes, a scattering of Freds, and one Charley.

And in a private room on the top floor, the Littlest Red Horse found the one he was seeking. He thought at first that the bed was unoccupied; but looking more closely he discovered there was a very small boy under the blanket.

"Hello," said the Littlest Red Horse. "Does your name by any chance happen to be 'Edward'?"

"Yes," answered the boy, "although almost everybody just says 'Eddie'."

"Well, I thought maybe I knew you."

"You're the first red horse I've ever seen," marvelled Eddie. "Does it hurt being red?"

"Certainly not! What do you think I am—sunburned?" The Littlest Red Horse was indignant.

The Littlest Red Horse's indignation turned to worry when he saw how pale and sad the little boy was. What could he do to make him happy? Finally the Littlest Red Horse said, "If I were you, I wouldn't stay here a minute."

"But I've got to stay." The boy's lower lip trembled. "You see—I'm sick."

"Oh, that's too bad. What's the name of your complaint?"

"I don't know. But it's something that makes the doctors shake their heads when they look at me, and my mother sleeps in that little bed in the corner every night."

"That sounds serious." The Littlest Red Horse felt Eddie's forehead with his nose to find out if the boy might be feverish. "I'm not an M.D., myself—but for self-protection, I've read enough books to qualify as an M.B.E."

"What's that?"

"Master Bug Exterminator. If you like, I can examine you for termites and Japanese beetles?"

"Well, thank you very much, Mr. Horse, but I'm sure it isn't either one of those."

"Oh." The Littlest Red Horse thought for a moment. "Tell me—were you ever in the Orient?"

"No—at least, I don't think so. I haven't been much of anywhere." Eddie turned his face toward the wall. "Nowhere but home and in this hospital. Where's the Orient?"

"Over yonder." The Littlest Red Horse gave an eastward switch with his tail. "The reason I asked is because I, myself, almost came down with a case of dry-rot after a trip over there. A Herr Schmidt owned the merry-go-round at that time."

"You mean—" the boy looked at the Littlest Red Horse with envy, "you mean that you work on a merry-go-round?"

"Yes, I do."

"That must be wonderful!"

"Well, it's nice work if you can get it," said the Littlest Red Horse nonchalantly. "Of course, you must be made of the best grade of hardwood when you have to support the crowned bottoms of Europe!"

"You mean you've been to Europe, too?"

"I've been everywhere! Around the world almost as many times as there are days in a month."

There was excitement in Eddie's eyes. "I just wish I could do things like that!"

"Well, why can't you?" exclaimed the Littlest Red Horse. "Come on— we'll go together and I'll point out all the places of interest."

"Oh, I can't." The boy's face fell. "I could never walk so far."

"Who said anything about you walking?" said the horse, in a tone that was half smile and half horse-laugh. "I've carried people of every size, shape, race, nationality, age, faith, party, sex, profession, and economic stratum—so I certainly shan't split or crack along my grain carrying you." He moved up close to the bed and tenderly said, "Come on, Eddie—climb on and let's get going!"

"Well, all right—if you're sure you don't mind, Mr. Horse," and he crawled out from under the covers and slid onto the back of the Littlest Red Horse.

"Now, let's see—where shall we go first? How about England?" said the Littlest Red Horse as he did a few merry-go-round circles around the room. "How would you like to see the Queen?"

"Oh, I'd like that—I've never seen one!" cried the boy. "But don't they keep her locked inside the castle so just anybody can't get in?"

"Naturally they keep her locked up!" answered the Littlest Red Horse. "Gates and doors and locks and bars—but they won't stop us! Just one good kick with my back legs and the gates will pop wide open! You'll see! We'll make headlines before you know it! Ready?"

"Ready, Mr. Horse!"

"Then here we go!" The Littlest Red Horse tossed his mane, arched his neck, and was off at a rolling gallop, his small hoofs moving in near perfect rhythm as though his cocked ears could hear the familiar strains of his merry-go-round organ.

And his prediction came true. They did make headlines all around the world!

Report of the Captain of the Guard, Buckingham Palace: "Received urgent summons to the bedchamber of Her Majesty at 2:00 a.m. She informed me that she had been awakened from a sound sleep by someone wearing wooden shoes trotting across her stomach, and the laughter of a small boy."

Report from the Paris chief of police: "Sometime during the night, a band of villains entered the Louvre by forcing the door with a battering ram studded with a horseshoe. No treasure of art is missing—but every canvas in which no horse was

depicted was turned to the wall!"

Bulletin posted by the dispatcher of the Red Top Gondola Company, Venice: "Until further notice, all gondoliers of this company will use bypass 101. A sea serpent has been reported swimming up and down the Grand Canal and it bears a hump on its back that resembles a small child. Like some birds, it can also imitate the human voice. After overtaking and passing Gondolier Romano, it called back to him, 'GET A HORSE!'"

A clock was striking twelve on Saturday night when the Littlest Red Horse put Eddie back in his hospital bed. "There, Eddie!" he said and trotted over to open the window.

"Mr. Horse—"

The boy's voice was so faint and weak that the Littlest Red Horse stopped in the middle of a front-hoofstand and came over to the bed to listen.

"Mr. Horse—could we go some place else to-night that is simply elegant?"

"I suppose so. Elegant like for instance?"

"Like for instance—" Eddie's eyes lighted for a brief second, "like for in-stance . . . no, no, we couldn't go there."

"We could so!" snorted the Littlest Red Horse. "I can take you anywhere you want to go!"

"But not to this place." The boy's words were so soundless that the Littlest Red Horse had to cup his tail behind his ear to hear. "People say it's so elegant that everyone tries to be good so they will get to go there someday."

"We'll get in all right." The Littlest Red Horse feinted with his left hind hoof and sneaked a haymaker with his right.

"What do they call it?"

"My mother calls it Heaven."

The Littlest Red Horse looked down at Eddie and gently said, "Maybe you're too tired to go anywhere else tonight. Maybe tomorrow night or the night after tomorrow night..."

"It's got to be tonight, Mr. Horse! Don't you understand? If there's anything you want terribly to do, you ought never to put it off—because something always happens—like you're too tired or it's raining or company comes or you haven't got the money or the one you were going with can't go. We've just got to go tonight, Mr. Horse, or maybe I won't ever go at all!"

Any lumberman would have said that the Littlest Red Horse was made of the driest hardwood—yet at this moment, two great sap tears rolled out of his eyes.

"Anything you say. Come on, tiny one—slide onto my back."

"Thank you, Mr. Horse!" It took Eddie several minutes to mount his steed. Once there, he had to hold onto the mane with both hands to stay in the saddle. "Do you really think we can get in?"

"Naturally. We got into Buckingham Palace and every place else, didn't we?"

"But there'll be great gates made out of solid gold!"

"Gates, doors, locks and bars—what does it matter? One kick of my heels and they'll fly wide open!"

The Littlest Red Horse tossed his mane, arched his neck, and was off at his easy, rolling gallop, his small hoofs beating out a perfect and tireless rhythm while his eyes searched the darkness of the night to find what all people of all faiths have sought for all the centuries—the shortest, swiftest, easiest, truest road to Heaven . . .

At four o'clock on Sunday morning, the truck of Esteban Gomez, bearing his dismantled merry-go-round from the carnival grounds, stopped at the town limits. Esteban felt, since fate had brought him again to the scene of his loss, that he should look once more for his Littlest Red Horse.

With flashlight in hand he walked along the edge of the road—and suddenly, in the round circle of feeble light, a familiar and beloved figure appeared. Esteban gathered the Littlest Red Horse to his ample chest, carried him to the truck, and held him while he drove with one arm cradled around his precious Littlest Red Horse.

When the merry-go-round was reassembled, Esteban's friends at the carnival gathered around to congratulate him on his good fortune and to learn what injuries the Littlest Red Horse had suffered during his exposure to the elements.

Not one scratch of paint was missing. Not one long hair was gone from the mane or tail. Not one nick or gouge was visible on the proud head, the sturdy body, or the fleet, tapering legs. Everyone breathed a sigh of relief. The Littlest Red Horse was just as he had always been.

Yet, when the merry-go-round organ was started and the Littlest Red Horse took his first mighty leap, a sudden and reverent hush came over the crowd. They all stared in silence, for everyone saw that while there were twenty-four horses on the merry-go-round, the Littlest Red Horse was the only one that had two back hoofs that were shod with solid gold.